Made in the USA
Monee, IL
14 August 2021

75686198R00073